This is the story of Jack Pott.

You can read a little or read a lot!

There's something else.

Can you guess what?

Throughout this book there's

a flowerpot to spot.

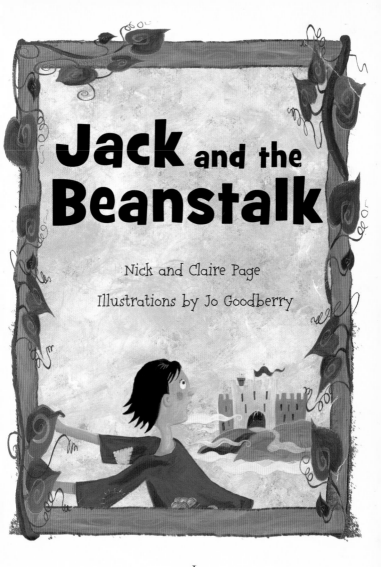

Jack and the Beanstalk

Nick and Claire Page

Illustrations by Jo Goodberry

make
believe
ideas

Jack Pott was very poor.
He lived in a shed with his
mother, Dotty, and a cow
called Skimmed Milk.

But Skimmed Milk wasn't giving
any milk. So Dotty sent Jack to sell
Skimmed Milk at the market.
Jack met a little old lady who said,
"Give me that cow and
I'll give you these
magic beans."
"Magic," said Jack.

Mother ~~Goose~~
Tradi~~tional~~
Fairy Tale
SEEDS
Magic
Beans
PACK of 5

"Mom!" said Jack. "Look what
I got for Skimmed Milk!"
Dotty could barely believe it.
"You jacket potato!" she said.
Dotty threw the beans out the
window and sent Jack to bed
without supper.
"You're grounded!" she said.

Next morning, it was dark outside.
Looking out, Jack saw why!
A big beanstalk had sprung up in the
garden and reached up to the sky.
"Now that's magic!" said Jack.

Jack decided to climb the beanstalk to see where it led. He climbed and clambered and clutched and clasped each branch, right to the top. And there, floating on a cloud, was a colossal castle. Jack darted through the double doors.

In the middle of a massive room
stood a tall table and chair.
"Someone BIG lives here," said Jack.
Then he saw a treasure chest
bursting with gold! Jack grabbed
the gold greedily and stuffed it
in his pockets.

Suddenly the door burst open
and a gigantic giant marched in.
He had a horrible head, enormous eyes,
nasty nostrils, terrible teeth, legs like
lampposts, and a bulging potbelly.
He was as tall as a tree and
as big as a bus!
"Now that's big!" said
Jack, as he tried to
hide inside the chest.

The giant stood still.
Then he roared:
"Fee fi fo fum,
I smell the blood
of an Englishman.
Be he alive or be he dead,
I'll grind his bones into
my bread."

Then the giant spotted Jack in the chest!
Jack jumped out, dodged between the
giant's long legs and ran. The giant
tripped and fell over with a terrible crash!

Jack ran out through the castle courtyard.
Behind him, he heard a rumbling roar:
"Fee fi fo fum,
I smell the blood of an Englishman.
When I nab this naughty knave,
I'll pop him in my microwave!"

Jack rushed to the beanstalk and climbed down as fast as he could. He slipped and slithered and skidded and slid. But the giant began to follow him down. Jack heard a rumbling roar:

"Fee fi fo fum,

I smell the blood of an Englishman.

I'll have him flattened, I'll have him fried,

I'll have boiled with a salad on the side!"

At the bottom of the beanstalk,

Jack's mother said, "You were grounded!"

"Get an axe!" said Jack.

"You mustn't play with axes!" said his mother.

"It's dangerous!"

"No," said Jack, pointing to the giant.

"That's dangerous!"

Jack and his mother heard a roar:
"Fee fi fo fum,
I smell the blood of
an English Mom!
I'll have her steamed,
I'll have her stewed,
I'll have her boiled or
barbecued!"

Jack's mother gave him the axe and he
started to chop the beanstalk. She even
took a turn with the bread knife.
Swing, swish, chop, chunk!

There was a creaking and a cracking and the
beanstalk fell like a toppled tree. Thump!
The giant fell to the ground, quite dead.
"Now that's grounded" said Jack.

The gold fell out of Jack's pockets.
"Look! Pots of money!" shouted Jack.
"We've hit the jackpot, Jack Pott!"
grinned his mother gleefully.
"But it was pot luck," said Jack.
"There'll never be another beanstalk."
"Hmmm . . . muttered his mom.

Jack bought back Skimmed Milk
from the little old lady. And Jack's mother
bought a big balloon and went on day trips.
But where she went, she never would say.

Ready to tell

Oh no! Some of the pictures from this story have been mixed up! Can you retell the story and point to each picture in the correct order?

Picture dictionary

Encourage your child to read these words from the story and gradually develop his or her basic vocabulary.

axe

beanstalk

castle

flowerpot

giant

market

mother

pointing

window

Key words

Here are some key words used in context. Help your child to use other words from the border in simple sentences.

They lived **in** a potting shed.

The cow was sold **at** the market.

He climbed **up** the beanstalk.

"**Look!**" said Jack.

They had lots **of** money.

Decorate a Dotty pot!

You may not be able to grow a giant beanstalk, but why not decorate a flowerpot and grow a plant of your own?

You will need
a medium-sized terracotta flowerpot and pot holder
- powder or poster paints in different colors
- craft glue • plastic cups • paintbrush

What to do
1 Make sure your flowerpot is clean and dry.
2 You are going to decorate the pot with paint mixed with craft glue. For each color mix $1/3$ glue to $2/3$ paint in a plastic cup. Use this to give the pot a waterproof and shiny "varnish" effect.
3 Paint the pot and holder with a base coat of one color and leave to dry.
4 When dry, use different colors to paint patterns on top of the base coat. You might like to make it as dotty as one of Dotty's dresses. Or you could paint it black and white like Skimmed Milk, the cow. Leave until dry.
5 Find out at your local garden center what will grow at this time of year. (Perhaps they will say "magic beans!") Follow their advice about how to plant the bulb or seeds they suggest.
6 Water the pot regularly and wait for the plant to grow.